HEY JACQUES, LET'S GO TO THE CAFE.

COPYRIGHT © MAIRA KALMAN 1988

ALL RIGHTS RESERVED

PRINTED IN THE UNITED STATES OF AMERICA ON ACID-FREE PAPER.

DESI

THIS IS A NEW YORK REVIEW BOOK PUBLISHED BY THE NEW YORK REVIEW OF BOOKS 435 HUDSON ST. NY, NY 10014 WWW.NYRB.COM ISBN 978-1-68137-168-9

AVAILABLE AS AN ELECTRONIC BOOK; ISBN 978-1-68137-169-6

A CATALOG RECORD FOR THIS BOOK IS AVAILABLE FROM THE LIBRARY OF CONGRESS.

SPECIAL WILLY THANKS TO K-K-KIKA

AND ALWAYS AND FOREVER TO MR. TIBOR AND DOS LOCOS BAMBINOS CON TODO MI AMOR

THANKS TO SEÑORA NANCY PAULSEN

FIRST PUBLISHED IN 1988

1 2 3 4 5 6 7 8 9 10

M + Co.

THIS BOOK IS FOR SARA AND SHOSHANA

HEY WILLY, SEE THE PYRAMIDS

by
MAIRA KALMAN

ALORS LOUIE, WHAT TIME IS IT?

The New York Review Children's Collection

Sometimes,
in the middle of the night,
when it is dark,
I call to my sister:
"Lulu, Lulu, Lulu.
Wake up. I can't sleep.
Tell me stories."
"Oh no," says Lulu
from far away, "not again,"
and shuffles over
to my bed.

She wiggles around,
gets comfortable,
sinks in.

"How many?" she says.
"A million?" I say.
"No," she says.
"Five?" I say.
"OK, five."

And Lulu begins.

big story

A very big woman
in a red dress
walked down the street
with three cross-eyed dogs.

When the dogs saw a yellow car
they started to bark.
The barking woke Aunt Ida,
who immediately started to sing.
The singing woke Uncle Morris,
who immediately started
to dance.

green hat

The three cross-eyed dogs
felt hungry.
They went to a fancy restaurant
and got a good table.

At the restaurant
a woman in a green hat
took a picture of a man
in a blue suit
while flowers sat
on the table
and smelled so sweet.

tiny story

Four very tiny people
walked right by me
on the way to school.
No one knew
where they were going,
but they were
walking very fast
and carrying
little instruments.

In front of
blue mountains
and green mountains
a thin skinny man
saw fish flying up.

Aunt Ida had a party.
The whole family was there.

Mr. Zelikovitch brought his son,
the genius, who was always
eating herring and
reading books.
Sara, the beauty, sat in the
middle of the room
peeling apples.
Leon brought ten warm cakes
and Aunt Rose wore her bathing suit,
because she swims in the ocean
every day.

The party was getting noisy.

Ida introduced
Ina to Ada,
Ada to Dada, and
Dada to Dudu.

Maishel Shmelkin,
our sweet neighbor next door,
walked into the room.
He was carrying a big
bouquet of cherry branches
but he forgot to wear his pants.

It was time
for the surprise.

"Please sit down,"
announced the man
in the red suit.
"I will sing a song
for you."

We clapped
and shouted bravo
and Jerome fell off his chair.

Am I sleeping?
Yes.
Am I dreaming?
Yes.
Did Mr. Zelikovitch bring his pet chicken?
Yes, he did.
Did Dada and Dudu wear hats?
Yes, pointy ones.
Did Maishel Shmelkin really forget
his pants?
Yes, it's true.
Could you tell me
more stories?

Shhh. Listen.

chicken story

A girl in a green dress
bought three oranges and a chicken
for dinner. Then she dressed
her brother neatly in red pants
and a little blue shirt. They
danced and danced until it
was late.

eddy and buddy

Eddy and Buddy the twins
had a party.
The room was a mess and
everything was
upside down.

A boy named Willy was
running around.

"Hey," said the boy,
"where's my shoe?
Hey," he said,
"I should have two."

tiptoe story

Aunt Ida and Uncle Morris had a dog
named Max.
Max wanted to live in Paris
and be a poet.
In the evening,
Max would tiptoe
down the hall, with a suitcase,
trying to sneak out of the house.
Ida would say to Morris,
"Quick, Morris,
catch the dog."

the poem of max

Max felt blue,
He went to the café
and ordered black coffee and biscuits.
He wrote down a poem
that went like this.

"Dig that boy
with the box
on his head.
Is he buying bread?
Is his name Fred?
And that tall noodle woman
with the polka-dot shoes—
have you ever seen
a nose so red?"

green face

My cousin Ervin
has a green face
and orange hair.
He is a scientist
and he told me about germs
and about something
that is called nothing.
His mother has very small ears
but she hears everything.

AND HE CAN FLY BACKWARDS AND HIS CAR GOES UPSIDEDOWN AND HIS WIFE SINGS IN OPERAS AND HIS SUN SEES PEOPLE FLOATING.

"What is nothing?" I ask.

"Nothing is when you are given
a very small portion of ice cream
by an adult,
and you look at the plate
and at the adult
and you ask for more
and the adult says
you have a huge portion
and you say
'That's it? That's nothing.'
"And that is nothing," says Lulu.

"I love Max the dog
and I will take him to Paris one day."

"I want to go to sleep, Alexander."

"Just one more story."

"And then,
good
night."

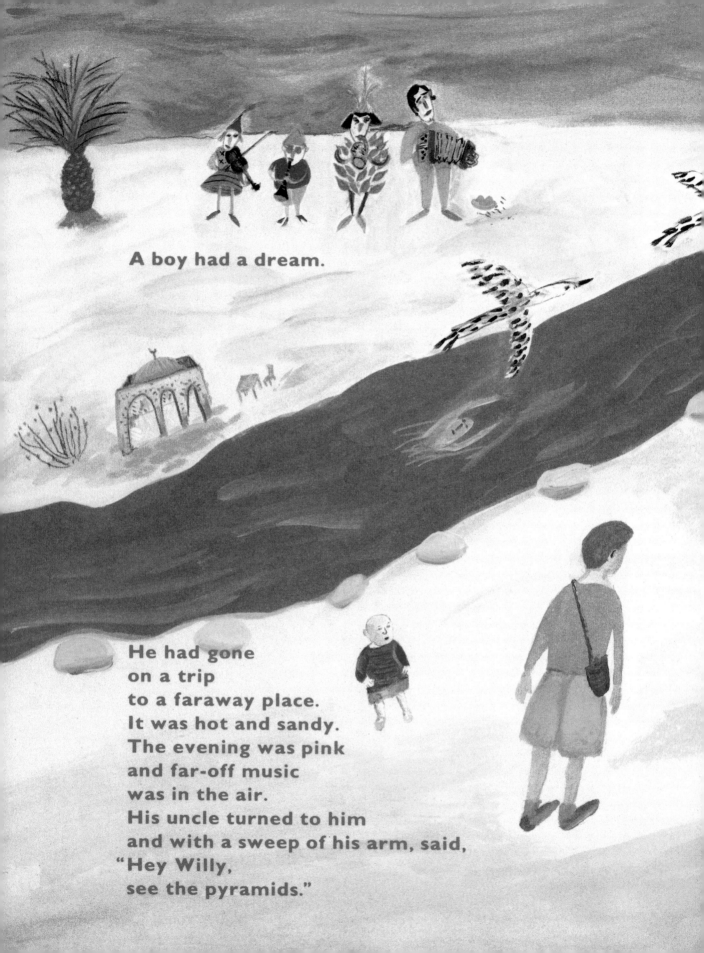

A boy had a dream.

He had gone
on a trip
to a faraway place.
It was hot and sandy.
The evening was pink
and far-off music
was in the air.
His uncle turned to him
and with a sweep of his arm, said,
"Hey Willy,
see the pyramids."

"The end," Lulu whispers.
I think I am asleep.
Then Lulu shuffles back
to her bed
and we both sink in
and see flying chairs
and green hats
and pink things
and sink some and
slowly sink
into sleep.